The Perfect Prince

by Paul Harrison
illustrated by Sue Mason

Evans

There was once a princess named Isabella. Like all princesses, she was expected to meet a handsome prince, fall in love and have a baby or two.

The Perfect Prince

For my nieces: Molly, Poppy, Maya and Isabella
from Paul

For Marlan & Hayley, with all my love.
Special thanks to dear Turps!
from Sue

First published 2008
Evans Brothers Limited
2A Portman Mansions
Chiltern Street
London W1U 6NR

British Library Cataloguing in Publication Data

Harrison, Paul, 1969-
   The perfect prince. - (Spirals)
   1. Children's stories
   I. Title
   823.9'2[J]

   ISBN-13: 9780237537715

Printed in China

Editor: Louise John
Design: Robert Walster
Production: Jenny Mulvanny

Unfortunately, Isabella didn't meet
any princes she liked.

"How about this one?" her mother, the
queen, would ask.

"No, not that one," she would reply.

She always said no. They were either too tall, or too small, or too fat, or too thin, or too clever, or too stupid, or too foolish, or too boring. They were never the perfect prince.

So Isabella went for long walks to avoid all the unsuitable suitors.

One day on her wanderings she came upon a frog.

Now, from the stories, she knew that when princesses kiss frogs there is a bit of magic and, hey-presto, the perfect prince appears in front of them.

So Isabella thought she'd
give it a go. She kissed the frog.
Nothing happened.
The frog didn't turn into a prince.
Instead it stayed just as froggy
as before.

14

By the time she got back home to
the palace, Isabella was looking
a little green.

"Are you well, dear?" asked her father,
the king.

"Croak," she replied.

"She must have a cold," said her
mother.

That night at supper,
Princess Isabella didn't
eat a thing.

Until she saw the fly. Out shot her tongue, and in went the fly.

"Oooh, disgusting!" said her mother.

"Yum!" thought Isabella.

Isabella was sent
straight to bed, so off
she hopped up the stairs.

23

That night strange things
happened in the palace.
Magical things.

25

In the morning, her parents came to wake her. But Isabella was nowhere to be seen.

Instead, in the middle of her bed, sat a frog.

"Yuck!" screamed the queen. "Get rid of that horrible creature!"

So the king threw
it out of the window.
It landed in the moat
with a plop.

But that frog was no ordinary frog. Of course, it was really Isabella.

Not that she could tell anyone who she really was. She could only croak.

Was she sad? Not at all. Being a frog meant no more soppy princes.

Instead she found her own perfect
prince – the frog she had kissed
the day before. Yes, he was
a bit green and ate flies all day
long, but so did Isabella now.
They fell in love and had
some babies.

About three thousand of them!